The
BEEZUS
and
RAMONA
Diary
BEVERLY
CLEARY

Illustrated by

Alan Tiegreen

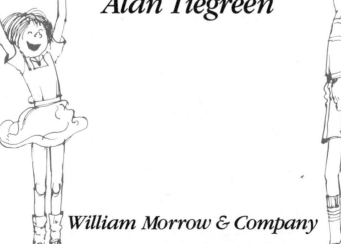

William Morrow & Company

New York

This diary belongs to

Elizabeth Rangel

Editorial services by Parachute Press, Inc.; book design by Ellen Friedman.
2 3 4 5 6 7 8 9 10

NEW DIARIES
FOR
BEEZUS
AND
RAMONA

Ramona was trying to tempt her older sister. "I'll let you read my diary if you'll let me read yours."

"No, thanks." Beezus hugged her diary to her chest.

This made Ramona sure her sister had written about boys, something she had suspected all along. However, even though she was curious, Ramona had not cheated by peeking into her sister's diary, not even once, even though she had been tempted many times. After all, she did not want anyone snooping in her diary. Fair was fair.

The two girls had written in their diaries, off and on, all year. Sometimes they wrote every day; sometimes they skipped a week or two, but every time they picked up their diaries and read over what they had written, they found they wanted to write more. They wrote happy, sad, and angry thoughts. They often discovered they felt better when they had finished.

Now the girls had come to the last page of the year. Beezus found a pen, and with it they took turns,

each solemnly signing the promise to keep her diary to read when she grew up.

"I'm glad Daddy brought us new diaries," said Ramona.

"Yes, I would miss having one." Beezus thumbed through the pages of the past year. "Some of the things I wrote the first of the year seem pretty funny now."

Ramona flipped through the pages of her now-grubby diary. "I used to spell *animal, a-m-i-n-a-l.* I wouldn't do that now." She wondered what Beezus had written about boys and if there was anything she could find to write about boys herself. There was that boy everyone called Yard Ape who chased her around the playground at school. She could write about how horrible he was.

Ramona went to work filling out the first part of her new diary, the part called *"ME" by Me,* before she turned to the first page of "January" and the space for writing five events she wished would happen in the coming year. She thought a moment before she wrote, "This year I am going to chase Yard Ape for a change. Ha-ha." Later in the diary, when she came to the secret code, she would write how she *really* felt about Yard Ape. The girls at school said boys were awful, but Yard Ape—well, Ramona was going to write about him in secret code to make sure no one would ever find out how she felt about him.

"ME" BY ME

My name is _Elizabeth Rangel_

At school my friends call me _Elizabeth_

I was born on _November 23, 1978_

My address is _768 Calle Corrilb_
San Dimas CA 91773

I have _Dark brown_ hair.
(give color)

It is curly/straight/wavy and it is short/medium/long.
(circle one)   (circle one)

I have _24_ teeth.
(give number)

I have _yellow-green_ -colored eyes.

I am _____ feet and _____ inches tall.

I weigh _____ pounds.

In my family I am the oldest/youngest/in the middle.
(circle one)

My brothers and sisters are named

Audrey

Our pets are named _Mimi (Dog)_

My best friend is Erin

My other friends are Kari,

My favorite book is Sweet Vally Twins

My favorite song is Time after time, Kokomo

My favorite food is Chicken, pizza

I go to school at Arcadia C. School

I'm in the 4th/5th grade.

I'm involved with these after-school activities:

playing, working, waiting for my mom

On school nights, I stay up until 8:30 o'clock.

On the weekend, I stay up until 9:30 o'clock.

JANUARY

Ramona's heart began to pound as if something exciting were about to happen.

Ramona and Her Father

January begins a new year. What excitement does the year hold for you?

I wish these five events would happen this year:

1. My Dog would to Talk

2.

3.

4.

5.

FEELING GROWN-UP

Mother laughed and looked at Beezus. "I'm afraid all we can do is wait for her to grow up," she said.

And when Mother said *we* like that, Beezus almost felt sorry for Ramona, because she would have to wait such a long time to be grown-up.

Beezus and Ramona

I feel grown-up when I: (Check the ones that are true for you and then add your own.)

☐ Get dressed up
☐ Go shopping alone
☐ Am given a hard job and do it
☐ Cook a meal
☐ Take care of a smaller child
☐ Help wash the car
☐ Help carry in groceries and put them away

☐ Or...

....

....

....

IF I COULD . . .

If I could take a trip anywhere in the world, here's where I'd like to go, what I would take with me, and what I think it would be like:

A SECRET CODE FOR SUPER SECRETS

Ramona and Beezus have a secret code. Here is how they write coded messages to one another.

The secret in this secret code is that only every third letter in the jumble of letters counts. For example, this is how Beezus would go about sending Ramona a coded message that said, "See you tonight."

First, she would write out her message, leaving enough room for two meaningless letters before the first letter *and* between every other letter—like this:

___S__E __E __Y__O __U
__T__O__N__I__G__H__T.

Then she would fill in the blank space with any letters that came into her head. When she finished, her message might look like this:

QWSEREYUE ZAYICOLPU
HJTXPOUINMNIDJGPLHNBT.

Ramona could decode this message by circling or underlining every third letter, as shown below.

QWSEREYUE ZAYICOLPU
HJTXPOUINMNIDJGPLHNBT.

You can change this code by simply changing how many letters come between the important letters. Instead of every third letter, you can make every second letter important, or every fourth.

If you want to make certain that this code stays secret, pull out this page and hide it in a safe place.

SECRETS

Mr. Quimby smiled at Ramona and rumpled her hair. "I doubt if anyone could figure out how you think," he said, which made Ramona feel better, as if her secret thoughts were still safe.

Ramona Quimby, Age 8

This is the biggest secret I am keeping right now: (You might want to use your secret code here.)................................

....

....

Here's what I think would happen if I told this secret:...

....

She was a girl who could not wait. Life was so interesting she had to find out what happened next.

Ramona the Pest

Beezus scowled. "I've been good old sensible Beezus all my life, and I'm tired of being sensible." She underlined this announcement by adding, "Ramona can get away with anything, but not me. No. I always have to be good, old, sensible Beezus."

Ramona and Her Mother

These are the ways I am sensible:

These are the ways I am not so sensible—according to other people!

"When will they be here?" asked Ramona Quimby, who was supposed to be dusting the living room but instead was twirling around trying to make herself dizzy. She was much too excited to dust.

Ramona and Her Mother

Once when I was excited because I was happy, this is what I did:

_____

_____

_____

_____

_____

_____

_____

_____

_____

_____

_____

"Don't worry, Mother," said Ramona. "I'm not going to school in my pajamas." As soon as she had spoken Ramona thought how pleasant it would be if she could go to school in her pajamas and feel the soft fuzz against her skin all day.

Ramona and Her Mother

Together the girls studied the pamphlet. Many names would not do at all. Philbert, which meant "superior," sounded good with Quimby, but at school, boys would call him a nut.

Ramona Forever

Some of the funny nicknames I hear around school are

If I could choose my own nickname, I would like it to be

GOOD NEWS

"Did Mrs. Rudge say anything about my spelling?" Ramona hesitated to ask the question, but she did want to know the answer.

"Why, no," said Mrs. Quimby. "She didn't even mention spelling, but she did say you were one of her little sparklers who made teaching interesting."

Ramona and Her Mother

Here's the best news I've heard recently:

....

....

....

This is good news I hope I'll hear soon:

....

....

....

My teacher likes/does not like me because
(circle one)

....

....

TALKING WITH A TEACHER

Her teacher seemed so kind, so soft and plump, that Ramona longed to lean against her and tell her all her troubles, how hot she was and how no one ever said she was her mother's girl and how she wanted her mother to love her like a little rabbit . . .

Ramona and Her Mother

My favorite teacher is...
....

If I could sit down and talk with him/her about everything, here is what I would say:............................

....

....

....

....

....

....

....

FUNNY TIME

This is something I saw that made me laugh:

JANUARY: LOOKING BACK

This is what made me happiest this month:

This is what made me the angriest:

I felt foolish when

This was the most exciting event of January:

These are the books I have read:

I liked these movies:

Here's what happened at an after-school event:

This is something new that I learned this month:

On a scale of one to ten, with ten being the best and one being the worst, I would rate this month a:

1 2 3 4 5 6 7 8 9 10

NEXT MONTH: LOOKING FORWARD

These are dates I want to remember next month:

Birthdays: ....

....

School events: ....

....

Holidays: ....

....

Other important dates: ....

....

This is something I'm looking forward to next month:

....

....

This is something coming up that I'm worried about:

....

....

This is something new I want to try next month: ....

....

....

FEBRUARY

VALENTINE'S DAY

This year I sent valentines to ....

....

....

I received valentines from ....

....

....

I do/don't think Valentine's Day is silly because.............
(circle one)

....

Glue or tape your favorite valentine here.

FRIENDLY FEELINGS

Beezus talked a long time on the telephone to a friend Ramona did not know. The conversation was about who said what to a new boy at school . . . and how some girl said she had seen some boy looking at Beezus, because Beezus said, "Do you think he looked at me, *really?*"

Ramona Forever

I think/wish that this boy/girl is interested in me:
(circle one)

I hope so/hope not because
(circle one)

SLEEPING OVER

Beezus was no help. She had spent the night at Mary Jane's house with several other girls, and they had stayed up late watching a horror movie on television and eating popcorn. Afterward they stayed awake talking, too scared to go to sleep.

Ramona Quimby, Age 8

Sometimes I spend the night at..

....

This is what we do there:...

....

....

....

....

Here's why I do/don't like staying there instead of at
(circle one)
my own home:...

....

LETTING OFF STEAM

She felt good from making a lot of noise, she felt good from the hard work of walking so far on her tin-can stilts, she felt good from calling a grown-up "pieface" and from the triumph of singing backward from ninety-nine to one. She felt good from being out after dark with rain on her face and the streetlights shining down on her.

Ramona and Her Father

This is what I do to get rid of bottled-up energy: (Check the ones that are true for you and then add your own.)

☐ Scream
☐ Sing loud
☐ Jump
☐ Dance
☐ Run
☐ Ride my bike
☐ Play a sport
☐ Exercise
☐ Telephone a friend
☐ Do cartwheels and somersaults

☐ Other ....

Surprised by sympathy from Yard Ape, Ramona reluctantly left the office. She expected him to go on ahead of her, but instead he walked beside her, as if they were friends instead of rivals. Ramona felt strange walking down the hall alone with a boy.

Ramona Quimby, Age 8

She knew exactly what she wanted to do and set about doing it. She worked with paper, crayons, Scotch tape, and rubber bands. She worked so hard and with such pleasure that her cheeks grew pink. Nothing in the whole world felt as good as being able to make something from a sudden idea.

Ramona Quimby, Age 8

This is something I created that I feel very proud of:

When Ramona left the shoe store with her beautiful red boots, *girl's* boots, in a box, which she carried herself, she was so filled with joy she set her balloon free just to watch it sail over the parking lot and up, up into the sky until it was a tiny red dot against the gray clouds.

Ramona the Pest

✧✳✧✳✧✳✧✳✧✳✧✳✧✳✧✳✧✳✧✳✧✳✧✳✧

Her mother was always saying everyone must be patient with Beezus when she was cross because Beezus had reached a difficult age, but what about Ramona? Her age was difficult, too . . .

Ramona and Her Mother

The most difficult thing about my age is

FUNNY TIME

This is something that happened in school that made me laugh:

....

....

....

....

....

....

....

....

....

....

....

....

....

DISASTER DAY

In February there came a day for Ramona when everything went wrong, one thing after another, like a row of dominoes falling over.

Ramona and Her Mother

I once had a day when something went wrong. This is what happened: ....

....

....

....

Here's something that went wrong in school not long ago: ....

....

....

....

One time I was just trying to be helpful and this is what went wrong: ....

....

....

IF I COULD

If the mayor asked me to run my neighborhood, this
is what I would change:

But this is something about my neighborhood that I
hope never changes:

On the way to the florist, the shoppers came to a ski goods store that was having a sale. "Just what your aunt and I need," said Uncle Hobart, leading the way among the racks of ski clothing, where he quickly bought quilted down jackets for himself and his bride, waterproof pants, fur-lined gloves, heavy socks, and boots, all great bargains. Fortunately, Beezus knew her aunt's sizes.

Ramona Forever

February is a good month for skiing, sledding, and skating!

My favorite winter sport is ....

....

....

The best time I had doing this was when ....

....

....

....

These are the clothes grown-ups make me wear outdoors to keep warm: ....

....

....

PROUD OF OUR PRESIDENTS

My school was closed for the birthdays of
☐ George Washington ☐ Abraham Lincoln
☐ Presidents' Day

This is what we did at school to celebrate their birthdays:

The president I admire most is

because

FEBRUARY: LOOKING BACK

Here's something that I wish I'd done differently this
month: ....

I'm proud of myself for doing this: ....
....

This is the song I liked best in February: ....
....

The best book I read this month was ....
....

The biggest news in school was ....
....

The person who annoyed me the most this month
was ....
because ....
....
....

The best surprise of this month was ....
....

On a scale of one to ten, I would rate this month a:
1   2   3   4   5   6   7   8   9   10

NEXT MONTH: LOOKING FORWARD

These are dates I want to remember next month:

Birthdays: ....

....

School events: ....

....

Holidays: ....

....

Other important dates: ....

....

This is something I'm looking forward to next month:

....

....

This is something coming up that I'm worried about:

....

....

This is something new I want to try next month: ....

....

MARCH

Ramona came to a halt at the intersection guarded by Henry Huggins in his yellow slicker, rain hat, and brown boots. "Look at all that nice mud," she said, pointing to the area that was to be the parking lot for the new market. It was such nice mud, rich and brown with puddles and little rivers in the tire tracks left by the construction trucks. It was the best mud, the muddiest mud, the most tempting mud Ramona had ever seen. Best of all, the day was so rainy there were no construction workers around to tell anyone to stay out of the mud.

"Come on, Howie," said Ramona. "I'm going to see how my boots work in the mud."

Ramona the Pest

According to the calendar, spring comes in March—but the cold, rain, and snow usually linger on.

This is what I like to do outdoors on rainy days: sit outside + watch rain

This is my favorite outdoor activity on snowy days: tubbing

This is how I feel on very windy days: cozy

THE MISCHIEF-MAKER IN ME

She had done something she had always wanted to do. *Of course* she would never squeeze out a whole tube of toothpaste again. She had done it once. She did not need to do it again.

Ramona and Her Mother

Something naughty I just couldn't resist doing once was

Doing it made me feel

Something I'd really love to do now but know I won't is

FRIENDS TO THE END

"Scooter McCarthy, you stop teasing Henry,"
said Beezus. "You're just jealous, because you
didn't win something like Henry did."

Henry and Beezus

Here's a time when I helped out a friend:......................

....

....

....

....

I was glad/sorry I did because...
    (circle one)

....

....

....

....

It made me feel good when a friend helped me in this

way:..

....

....

....

SCHOOL'S IN

She loved Miss Binney for not being cross when she was late for school. She loved Miss Binney for telling her she was a brave girl.

Ramona the Pest

This is my idea of a perfect teacher:

The nicest compliment a teacher ever gave me was

PICTURE THIS

She blinked away the tears and discovered on her bedside table a cartoon her father had drawn for her. It showed Ramona leaning against one tree and the family's car leaning against another. He had drawn her with crossed eyes and a turned-down mouth. The car's headlights were crossed and its front bumper turned down like Ramona's mouth. They both looked sick. Ramona discovered she remembered how to smile.

Ramona Quimby, Age 8

Describe how you felt when you were sick and draw a picture of yourself feeling that way.

_____

_____

_____

_____

_____

_____

_____

HAPPY HOURS

This time Ramona did not mind when her mother laughed. She laughed a bit, too . . .

Ramona and Her Mother

This made me feel really happy:

Here's what I did to show how I felt:

When this first happened, I didn't think it was one bit funny:

But now that I look back at it, it *was* pretty funny because

IF I COULD . . .

Ramona liked good lively comedies with lots of children and animals and grown-ups doing silly things. Next to that she liked cat food commercials.

Ramona the Brave

If I could make up my own television show, this is

what it would be like:

If I could change something about my favorite tele-

vision show, _____, this is what
(name of show)

I would change:

Agreeing with Beezus—Beatrice—gave Ramona a cozy feeling, as if something unusually pleasant had taken place.

Ramona the Brave

Ramona had two feelings about this conversation. She did not want her father's hair to grow thin or her mother's hair to grow gray. She wanted her parents to stay exactly as they were for ever and ever. But, oh, how good it was to see them be so affectionate with one another.

Ramona Quimby, Age 8

◎◎◎◎◎◎◎◎◎◎◎◎◎◎◎◎◎◎◎◎◎◎◎◎◎◎◎◎◎◎

. . . she found the hidden key, let herself in the back door, washed her hands, ate an apple, put the core in the garbage, changed from school clothes into old jeans and a T-shirt, and sat down on the couch to read. She felt grown-up and very, very good.

Ramona Forever

Then Ramona felt her mother's hand on her back. "Ramona," she said gently, "what are we going to do with you?"

With red eyes, a swollen face, and a streaming nose, Ramona sat up and glared at her mother. "Love me!"

Ramona the Brave

If I ever have a son or a daughter I will always

And I will never

GOOD NEWS

Here's the best news I've heard recently:

This is good news I hope I'll hear soon:

FAMILY FLARE-UPS

"The funniest thing happened at school," said Beezus, and Ramona understood that her sister was anxious to start a conversation that would smooth things over and make their parents forget their quarrel, perhaps make them laugh.

Ramona and Her Mother

This is what I do when my parents argue: (Check the ones that are true for you.)

☐ Interrupt to change the subject
☐ Feel sick inside
☐ Stay quiet
☐ Go to my room
☐ Get angry, too
☐ Hide
☐ Go outside
☐ Cry
☐ Figure it will pass
☐ Turn on the TV
☐ Cover my ears
☐ Tell them to stop
☐ Other

MARCH: LOOKING BACK

This is what made me laugh the hardest this month:

....

....

This is what made me the angriest: ....

....

I felt foolish when ....

....

This was the most exciting event in March: ....

....

These are the books I read: ....

....

....

I enjoyed this movie: ....

Here's what happened at an after-school event: ....

....

This is something new that I learned this month: ....

....

On a scale of one to ten, I would rate this month a:

1   2   3   4   5   6   7   8   9   10

NEXT MONTH: LOOKING FORWARD

These are dates I want to remember next month:

Birthdays: ....

....

School events: ....

....

Holidays: ....

....

Other important dates: ....

....

....

This is something I'm looking forward to next month:

....

....

This is something coming up that I'm worried about:

....

....

This is something new I want to try next month: ....

....

....

APRIL

A warm misty rain was falling. Bits of green tipped the black branches of trees. Ramona slowed down to investigate crocus buds like tiny yellow and blue Easter eggs that were pushing up through a neighbor's lawn.

Ramona and Her Mother

April is a new beginning. The grass turns green and flowers appear. It is the time of baby animals, too.

My favorite flower is

The bird I like best is the

I think the prettiest tree is the

This is what I enjoy most about the coming of spring:

A WALK IN SPRING

Take a walk and look around your neighborhood for a sign of spring. Write a poem about it or draw a picture of what you find.

FEELING GREAT!

On the way to school Ramona cut across the
lawn for the pleasure of leaving footprints in
the dew.

Ramona and Her Father

Here are some things I like to do in the spring:

☐ Splash in puddles
☐ Kick cans
☐ Watch birds
☐ Look at new flowers and buds
☐ Get muddy
☐ Walk in the rain
☐ Stop wearing my winter clothes

☐ And

AWFUL SECRET

"Beezus, you look as if something is bothering you," remarked Aunt Beatrice.

Beezus looked down at her plate. How could she ever tell such an awful thing?

"Why don't you tell us what is wrong?" Aunt Beatrice suggested. "Perhaps we could help."

Beezus and Ramona

I once had an awful secret and I told about it. I felt better/worse.
(circle one)

This is something I'm afraid to share now: (You can write it in code.)

Someone I could talk to about it is

DREAMLAND

"Mama, I had a bad dream last night."
"What did you dream?"
"Something was chasing me, and I couldn't run."
The dream was still vivid in Ramona's mind.

Ramona the Brave

Here's a dream I had that is still vivid in my mind:

....

....

....

....

....

My weirdest dream was...

....

....

....

....

MONEY MATTERS

She had never thought what it might be like not to have enough money—not that the Quimby's ever had money to spare. . . . As she laid out knives and forks, Ramona wondered how she could earn money, too.

Ramona and Her Father

My family does/does not worry about money. This
(circle one)

makes me feel ....

....

....

Here's how I get my spending money: ....

....

....

This is what I spend it on: ....

....

....

I sometimes earn money by ....

....

....

If I earned a million dollars, this is what I would do with it:

The rain finally stopped. Ramona watched for dry spots to appear on the sidewalk and thought of her roller skates in the closet.

Ramona Quimby, Age 8

Ramona knew that taxes were something unpleasant that worried parents. "I think you should stop paying taxes," Ramona informed her mother.

Ramona Quimby, Age 8

By the time Ramona reached the corner, she was less wobbly. She even managed to turn the corner without tipping over. She began to pedal faster. Now she was really riding, filled with joy, as if she were flying.

Ramona Forever

The first time I rode a bicycle/roller-skated/swam
(circle one)

I felt

Mrs. Quimby then spoke the most beautiful words Ramona had ever heard, "Oh, Ramona, how I've missed you."

Ramona Forever

I DON'T FEEL WELL . . .

She longed for her mother, and suddenly, as if her wish were granted, her mother was entering the bedroom with a basin of water and a towel.

"Mother!" croaked Ramona. "Why aren't you at work?"

"Because I stayed home to take care of you," Mrs. Quimby answered, as she gently washed Ramona's face and hands. "Feeling better?"

Ramona Quimby, Age 8

The last time I was sick I had

The sickest I've ever been was when I

This is what I hate most about being sick:

The only good part about being sick is

SCHOOL'S IN

When lunchtime came, Ramona collected her lunch box and went off to the cafeteria where, after waiting in line for her milk, she sat at a table with Sara, Janet, Marsha, and other third-grade girls.

Ramona Quimby, Age 8

At lunchtime I bring my own lunch/eat at the cafeteria. My favorite lunch is
(circle one)

I sit with these friends:

We usually talk about

SHOWING OFF

Mrs. Whaley's smile was mischievous. "Tell me, Ramona," she said, "don't you ever try to show off?"

Ramona was embarrassed. "Well. . . maybe . . . sometimes, a little," she admitted.

Ramona Quimby, Age 8

I have never/maybe once/maybe more tried to show
(circle one)

off. ....

The time I was most embarrassed after showing off

was ....

....

....

....

The funniest time was ....

....

....

....

APRIL: LOOKING BACK

Here's something that I wish I'd done differently this
month:

I'm proud of myself for doing this:

This is the song I liked best in April:

The best book I read this month was:

The biggest news in school was:

The person who made me the happiest this month
was

because

The best surprise of this month was

On a scale of one to ten, I would rate this month a:

1   2   3   4   5   6   7   8   9   10

NEXT MONTH: LOOKING FORWARD

These are dates I want to remember next month:

Birthdays: ....

....

School events: ....

....

Holidays: ....

....

Other important dates: ....

....

This is something I'm looking forward to next month:

....

....

This is something coming up that I'm worried about:

....

....

This is something new I want to try next month: ......

....

....

"Hello, Henry," said Beezus, gathering a handful of tulip petals and tossing them into the air so they fell over her in a pink shower.

Henry and Beezus

S pring is a time for flowers, sunshine, and special friends.

When I like someone, this is how I feel inside: ....

....

....

This is what I do: ....

....

....

The boy/girl I like best now is ....
(circle one)

I know that person does/doesn't feel the same way about
(circle one)

me because ....

....

....

When I was younger, I had a big crush on: ....

....

....

BIRTHDAY PARTIES

"What would you like to do to celebrate your birthday next week?"

Beezus thought a minute. "Well . . . I'd like to have Aunt Beatrice over for dinner. She hasn't been here for such a long time. And I'd like to have a birthday cake with pink frosting."

Beezus and Ramona

The best birthday I ever had was ....

....

....

Someday I would like to celebrate my birthday in this

way: ....

....

....

....

....

....

....

NO FAIR!

"You always get your own way, because you're the youngest." . . . And that's not fair, thought Beezus. Ramona shouldn't get her own way when she had been naughty.

Beezus and Ramona

This is something really unfair that happened recently:

SCHOOL'S OUT

Beezus and Ramona both looked forward to Friday afternoons after school.

Beezus and Ramona

This is what I do on Fridays after school:
- ☐ Go home
- ☐ Go to a friend's house
- ☐ Go to a relative's house
- ☐ Go to a lesson
- ☐ Go to a club meeting
- ☐ Hang around the school yard

This is an after-school activity that I am involved in:

....

....

....

....

The part of the weekend I like best is ....

....

....

....

MY MOM

"I couldn't get along without my Ramona," said Ramona's mother. She held out her arms. Ramona ran into them. Her mother had said the words she had longed to hear. Her mother could not get along without her. She felt warm and safe and comforted and oh, how good her mother smelled, so clean and sweet like flowers. Better than any mother in the whole world.

Ramona and Her Mother

If I had to describe my mother in five words, those words would be:

A time I felt particularly close to my mother was when:

Sunday morning Ramona and Beezus were still resolved to be perfect until dinnertime. They got up without being called, avoided arguing over who should read Dear Abby's advice first in the paper, complimented their mother on her French toast, and went off through the drizzly rain to Sunday school neat, combed, and bravely smiling.

Ramona Quimby, Age 8

Sundays are different from other days of the week because

At our house this is what we usually do on Sunday:

"I like it when you stay home," she remarked, thinking of the days before her mother had gone to work when the house had smelled of baking cookies or homemade bread on Saturday morning.

Ramona and Her Mother

Ramona and Beezus, excited and frightened, looked at one another. At last! The fifth Quimby would soon be here. Nothing would be the same again, ever.

Ramona Forever

I wish/don't wish I had a brother or sister because............
(circle one)

Yard Ape—well, he was a problem, but so far she had not let him get the best of her for keeps. Besides, although she might never admit it to anyone, now that she had her eraser back she liked him—sort of. Maybe she enjoyed a challenge.

Ramona Quimby, Age 8

FUNNY TIME

Here's something I saw that made me laugh:.....................
....
....
....
....
....
....

IF I COULD . . .

If I could write a book when I grow up, this is what

it would be about:

PICTURE THIS

Beezus's unhappy mood disappeared as she swooped up Picky-picky, the Quimbys' shabby old cat, who had strolled into the kitchen.

Ramona and Her Father

Describe and draw a picture of your pet or an animal who lives in your neighborhood.

....

....

....

....

SECRETS

"Well, Ramona, suppose you tell me about what went on at school today," said Mr. Quimby with that false cheerfulness grown-ups use when they are trying to persuade children to tell something they don't want to tell.

Ramona the Pest

My friend told me this secret:

I did/did not keep the secret to myself because
(circle one)

One time I kept a secret, but felt better after I told it to someone. This is what happened:

The biggest secret I was ever asked to keep was

MAY: LOOKING BACK

This is what made me laugh the hardest this month:

....

This is what made me the angriest:.......................................

....

I felt foolish when...

....

This was the most exciting event of May:.............................

....

These are the books I read:..

....

I enjoyed these movies:..

....

Here's what happened at an after-school event:.................

....

This is something new that I learned this month:...............

....

....

On a scale of one to ten, I would rate this month a:

1   2   3   4   5   6   7   8   9   10

NEXT MONTH: LOOKING FORWARD

These are dates I want to remember next month:

Birthdays: ....

....

School events: ....

....

Holidays: ....

....

Other important dates: ....

....

This is something I'm looking forward to next month:

....

....

This is something coming up that I know I'll be good

at: ....

....

This is something new I want to try next month: ....

....

JUNE

Mrs. Quimby lifted wreaths of tiny pink roses from the florist's box, anchored them firmly to her daughters' hair with bobby pins before she handed them their nosegays. Both girls inhaled the fragrance of their flowers. "Ah-h."

Ramona Forever

June is the month of weddings and other special occasions.

I have been involved in these special events:

☐ Weddings
☐ Baptisms
☐ Bar Mitzvahs
☐ Bas Mitzvahs
☐ Birthday parties
☐ Graduation ceremonies
☐ Funerals
☐ Confirmations

☐ Others

This is the kind of party I enjoy most:

FRIENDS TO THE END

Beezus, seeing that Henry wanted to be alone, decided it was time to go home.

Henry and Beezus

A time when a friend of mine was very sensitive to my feelings was when ....

....

....

....

When one of my friends is sad, this is what I do: ....

....

....

....

One time a friend and I spent a great day together. This is what we did: ....

....

....

SCHOOL'S IN

Ramona dreaded school because she felt Mrs. Griggs did not like her, and she did not enjoy spending the whole day in a room with someone who did not like her, especially when that person was in charge.

Ramona the Brave

Sometimes I dread going to school because ....

....

....

....

....

I think my teacher likes/doesn't like me because ....
(circle one)

....

....

....

....

I wish my teacher would tell me ....

....

....

....

The newlyweds, both laughing, ran out to Uncle Hobart's truck in a shower of rice and birdseed and drove off. Two pairs of white slippers danced from the rear bumper. The wedding was over.

Ramona Forever

Once I went to a wedding and this is what happened:

....

....

....

....

....

"That's right," agreed her mother. "You will be my middle child, with a special place right in the middle of my heart."

Ramona Forever

This is something I wish my mother would say to me:

_____

_____

_____

_____

_____

_____

_____

_____

_____

_____

If there was one thing Ramona couldn't stand,
it was being ignored.

Beezus and Ramona

Maybe grown-ups weren't perfect, but they should be, her parents most of all. They should be cheerful, patient, loving, never sick, and never tired. And fun, too.

Ramona and Her Mother

IF I COULD . . .

If I could meet anyone in the whole world, this is who it would be and here's what I would like to happen:

....

....

....

....

....

....

....

....

....

....

....

....

....

....

FATHER'S DAY

Hearing her father speak this way, as if she really was a grown-up, melted the last of Ramona's anger. . . . After a few moments of silence, she whispered, "I love you, Daddy."

Ramona and Her Father

This is what I like about my father:

☐ He takes me places   ☐ He's smart
☐ He talks to me   ☐ He's funny
☐ He cooks   ☐ He can fix things
☐ He's nice to my mother   ☐ He tells good stories
☐ He's nice to me   ☐ And ....
☐ He helps me
    with my homework

I don't like these habits my father has:

☐ He smokes   ☐ He works too hard
☐ He nags   ☐ He drives too fast
☐ He yells   ☐ He's always tired
☐ He sulks   ☐ He stays out late
☐ He criticizes   ☐ And ....

The nicest time I ever spent with my father was when..
....
....
....
....
....
....
....
....
....
....
....
....
....

HAPPY HOURS

This made me feel really happy:..

....

....

....

Here's what I did to show how good I felt:..................................

....

....

....

....

....

MY RELATIVES

She was *glad* she didn't have an Uncle Hobart. She was *glad* she didn't have any uncles at all, just Aunt Beatrice, who never embarrassed children and who always came when the family needed her.

Ramona Forever

The relative I like the most is

because

The relative I like least is

because

JUNE: LOOKING BACK

Here's something that I wish I'd done differently this month:

I'm proud of myself for doing this:

This is the song I liked best in June:

The best book I read this month was

The biggest news in school was

The person who pleased me most this month was

because

The best surprise of this month was

On a scale of one to ten, I would rate this month a:

1   2   3   4   5   6   7   8   9   10

NEXT MONTH: LOOKING FORWARD

These are dates I want to remember next month:

Birthdays:

School events:

Holidays:

Other important dates:

This is something I'm looking forward to next month:

This is something coming up that I'm worried about:

This is something new I want to try next month:

JULY

"Five double scoops of chocolate mandarin-orange dipped in nuts," was Uncle Hobart's order.

Double scoops with nuts. Beezus and Ramona were impressed.

Ramona Forever

Ice cream tastes so good during the hot, lazy days of summer.

This summer I plan to spend my time:

☐ Going to the beach   ☐ Training my dog
☐ Earning extra money   ☐ Skateboarding
☐ Riding my bike   ☐ Gardening
☐ Chasing fireflies   ☐ Putting on plays
☐ Going on picnics   ☐ At day camp
☐ Reading   ☐ At sleep-away camp
☐ Sewing   ☐ With my relatives
☐ Learning to cook

☒ Other Vacation to Hawaii

This is what I like best about summer:
Time off of school

ME ON THE OUTSIDE

Denise lifted locks of wet hair between her fingers and snipped with flying scissors. Lift and snip, all the way around Ramona's head. Flicks of a comb, and Denise aimed a hand-held hair dryer at Ramona's head with one hand while she guided Ramona's hair into place with a brush held in the other. In no time Ramona's hair was dry. More flicks of the comb, the plastic sheet was whisked away, and there sat Ramona with shining hair neatly shaped to her head.

Ramona and Her Mother

This is who usually cuts my hair:

Susan or Melony

This is how I wear my hair now:

down, ½ up or french braid

Once I got a haircut I hated, and this is what I did:

I got a haircut *
I hated it so I
went in & got a diffen
style

Use the space below to draw a picture of yourself wearing a brand new hairstyle. Or find a picture in a magazine of a hairstyle you'd like to try. Tape it in here.

ME ON THE INSIDE

Beezus watched Ramona eating her cold mashed potatoes and jelly and thought how much easier things would be now that she could look at her sister when she was exasperating and think, Ha-ha, Ramona, this is one of those times when I don't have to love you.

Beezus and Ramona

One time I didn't love my mother, father, sister, brother, or friend was when they did something mead mean to me

A time I don't think they loved me was when they yeal

GROWING UP

She thought vaguely of all the exciting things she would like to do—learn to twirl a lariat, play a musical saw, flip around and over bars in a gymnastic competition while crowds cheered.

Ramona Quimby, Age 8

This is how I imagine my life will be when I grow up:

Here is an adventure I'd like to have:

Go all around the world

Ramona made up her mind to shock her parents, really shock them. "I am going to run away," she announced.

"I'm sorry to hear that," said Mr. Quimby as if running away were a perfectly natural thing to do.

Ramona and Her Mother

A girl who was a sparkler needed a name that looked like a sparkler. And that was the way Ramona Quimby was going to write her name.

Ramona and Her Mother

Sometimes Ramona Quimby makes the *Q* in her name look like a cat's face, and sometimes she puts sparkle signs around the tail of the *y*. Write your name and show how you like to dress it up:

Elizabeth Rangel

. . . she was happy to see Howie coming down the street, wheeling his bicycle with his unicycle balanced across the seat and handlebars. She was even happier when he laid both on her driveway. Ramona met him at the door.

"Come on out, Ramona," said Howie. "Uncle Hobart helped me learn to ride my unicycle, so now you can ride my bicycle."

Ramona's wish had come true.

Ramona Forever

Ramona settled herself at the kitchen table with paper and crayons to draw a picture of the cat on the label of a can of Puss 'n Boots cat food. Ramona loved that jaunty booted cat, so different from old Picky-picky, who spent most of his time napping on Beezus's bed.

Ramona the Brave

Ramona blissfully read herself off into the land of princesses, kings, and clever youngest sons, satisfied that the Quimbys had a clever younger daughter who was doing her part.

Ramona Quimby, Age 8

NO FAIR!

But as Beezus held her facecloth under the
faucet she was not at all sure she would feel
better. For Ramona to spoil one birthday cake
was bad enough, but *two*. . . . Probably nobody else in the whole world had a little sister who had spoiled two birthday cakes on the
same day.

Beezus and Ramona

Someone spoiled my day once by

I felt bad because

This is what finally happened:

FORGIVE AND FORGET

When they had finished their pears with apricot jam, Ramona gave her mother a shy smile.

Mrs. Quimby smiled back and patted Ramona's hand. Ramona felt much lighter. Without using words, she had forgiven her mother for the unfortunate egg, and her mother had understood. Ramona could be happy again.

Ramona Quimby, Age 8

The time it was very hard for me to forgive someone was when ....

....

....

....

....

Here's what finally happened: ....

....

....

....

JULY: LOOKING BACK

This is what made me laugh the hardest this month:

a little girl named laura

This is what made me the angriest:

when J.B. hated me

I felt foolish when _I hated S.B._

This was the most exciting event of July: _25th_

Disneyland

These are the books I read:

I enjoyed these movies:

This is something new that I learned this month:

On a scale of one to ten, I would rate this month a:

1   2   3   4   5   6   7   (8)   9   10

NEXT MONTH: LOOKING FORWARD

These are dates I want to remember next month:

Birthdays:..

....

School events:...

....

Holidays:...

....

Other important dates:...

....

This is something I'm looking forward to next month:

....

....

This is something coming up that I'm worried about:

....

....

This is something new I want to try next month:

....

....

AUGUST

Friends had gone off to camp, to the mountains, or the beach. Howie and Willa Jean had gone to visit their other grandmother.

"Girls, please stop moping around," said Mrs. Quimby.

"We can't find anything to do," said Beezus.

Ramona Forever

Many people go on vacation in August. Those who stay home must find new things to do without their friends. When my friends are gone and there is no one to play with, this is what I do to amuse myself: ....

....

....

This is a trip I once went on in the summer: ....

....

....

Here's a summer vacation I dream of taking someday: ....

....

MY NEIGHBORHOOD

"Mrs. Swink is pretty old," volunteered Ramona. Mrs. Swink was a widow who lived in the house on the corner and drove an old sedan that Mr. Quimby admiringly called a real collector's item.

Ramona and Her Father

My favorite neighbor is .... because

....

....

The meanest neighbor is .... because

....

....

The strangest neighbor is .... because

....

....

The friendliest neighbor is .... because

....

....

....

HAPPY HOURS

This made me feel really happy: ....

....

....

....

Here's what I did to show how good I felt: ....

....

....

The house was quiet. Ramona worked happily, humming a tune from a television commercial. She used a pencil to draw cat fur, because she could draw finer lines with it than she could with a crayon.

Ramona the Brave

Ramona began to draw a fancy border, all scallops and curliques, around her name. She was happy, too, because her family had been happy that morning and because she was big enough for her family to depend on.

Ramona Quimby, Age 8

They would be disappointed in Ramona, that's what they'd be, and nothing made Ramona feel worse than knowing that her parents were disappointed in her.

Ramona the Brave

At playtime the whole class turned into Billy Goats Gruff and trip-trapped around the playground, but none so joyfully or so noisily as Ramona.

Ramona the Pest

Except for washing the egg beater in sudsy water so she could beat up a lot of suds, Ramona did not care much for housework, and this morning she longed to be outside racing up and down the sidewalk on her roller skates.

Ramona and Her Mother

A MIND FOR MANNERS

"Ramona, try to hold your fork properly," said her father. "Don't grip it with your fist. A fork is not a dagger."

With a small sigh, Ramona changed her hold on the fork. Grown-ups never remembered the difficulty of cutting meat when one's elbows were so far below the tabletop.

Ramona Quimby, Age 8

These are manners that my parents insist on:

I always get in trouble for forgetting:

This rule of manners makes no sense to me:

I think this is the most important rule of manners:

Here is something I wish grown-ups would remember when dealing with children:

FUNNY TIME

This is something a friend of mine did that made me

laugh:...

....

....

....

....

....

....

THE MISCHIEF-MAKER IN ME

"Ramona," said Mother quietly, "you may go to your room until you can behave yourself."

Beezus and Ramona

When I'm punished, I am:

☐ Sent to my room
☐ Spanked
☐ Not allowed to watch TV
☐ Not allowed to play with a friend

☐ Given extra chores, such as ....

....

....

☐ Other ....

....

....

The punishment I hate most is ....

....

....

The one I think is the most fair is ....

....

....

AUGUST: LOOKING BACK

Here's something that I wish I'd done differently this month:

I'm proud of myself for doing this:

This is the song I liked best in August:

The best book I read this month was

The person who annoyed me the most this month was

because

The best surprise of this month was

On a scale of one to ten, I would rate this month a:

1   2   3   4   5   6   7   8   9   10

NEXT MONTH: LOOKING FORWARD

These are dates I want to remember next month:

Birthdays: ....

....

School events: ....

....

Holidays: ....

....

Other important dates: ....

....

This is something I'm looking forward to next month:

....

....

This is something coming up that I'm worried about:

....

....

This is something new I want to try next month: ....

....

SEPTEMBER

As Ramona approached her bus stop, she thought about one of the best parts of her new school: none of her teachers in her new school would know she was Beatrice's little sister. Teachers always liked Beezus; she was so prompt and neat. When both girls had gone to Glenwood School, Ramona often felt as if teachers were thinking, I wonder why Ramona Quimby isn't more like her big sister.

Ramona Quimby, Age 8

S chool starts in September. It's a new beginning.

The best thing about this new school year is ....

....

I am/am not "prompt and neat" with my school work.
(circle one)
I think this is the reason why: ....

....

This is what I would like to do differently this school

year from what I did last year: ....

....

....

....

SCHOOL'S IN . . . AGAIN!

Beezus went off to her room, eager to do her homework on the new-to-her desk.

Ramona the Brave

Here are the clothes and school supplies that were new this school year: ....

....

Here's something I received that is not exactly new, but it's new to me: ....

....

On the first day of school I wore ....

....

I was glad to see these friends from last year: ....

....

My new teacher is ....

The first thing he/she said to the class was ....

....

....

....

This is what we did on the first day of school:

To me, the best thing about school is

The worst thing is

IF I COULD . . .

If I could be in charge of my school (and didn't have to worry about getting into trouble) this is what I'd do:

....

....

....

....

....

....

....

....

PICTURE THIS

She got down on her hands and knees and
went to work on the bedroom floor, printing
a sign in big letters.

Ramona and Her Father

Think of a message that you would like to get across to your
family. Then print it on a big piece of paper and pin it up
where everyone can see it.

This is what my sign said: ....

....

....

This is what my family said about it: ....

....

....

....

....

....

....

....

FAMILY FLARE-UPS

The Quimbys said very little at breakfast the next morning. Beezus was moody and silent.

Ramona and Her Father

When members of my family disagree, this is usually what we disagree about: (Check the ones that are true for you and then add your own.)

☐ What television show to watch
☐ Obeying my parents' rules
☐ Someone coming home late
☐ Someone making noise
☐ Money matters
☐ Someone making a mess
☐ Someone being rude
☐ Homework
☐ Sharing clothes
☐ Sharing toys and books
☐ Someone being a pest
☐ Housework
☐ And

The members of my family who disagree the most
are...

....

....

I think this may be because...

....

....

When I disagree with someone in my family this is
how it makes me feel:..

....

....

....

....

....

....

....

....

FRIENDLY FEELINGS

He was the only boy in the class in short pants, and Ramona liked him at once. She liked him so much she decided she would like to kiss him.

Ramona the Pest

The nicest girl in my class is Erin

The nicest boy is Jonathan

The student I would like to get to know this year is

I think it would be nice to know him or her better because

If someone in my class tried to kiss me when the teacher wasn't looking, I would tell

I imagine the rest of the class would laugh

How could she stay out of mix-ups when she
never knew what would suddenly turn into a
mix-up?

Ramona the Brave

✦✦

Beezus arrived first with an armload of books that she dropped on a chair. "Homework!" she said and groaned. Now that she was in junior high school, she was always talking about all the work she had to do, as if Ramona did nothing in school.

Ramona Quimby, Age 8

Ramona always longed for glorious surprises.
That was the way she was.

Ramona the Brave

The most glorious surprise I ever had was the time

Being such a bad, terrible, horrid, wicked girl made her feel *good*! She brought both heels against the wall at the same time. Thump! Thump! Thump! She was not the least bit sorry for what she was doing. She would *never* be sorry. Never! Never! Never!

Ramona the Pest

Raindrops began to dot the driveway, and tears dotted Ramona's skirt. She put her head down on her knees and cried.

Ramona and Her Father

DREAMLAND

Here's a dream I had that is still vivid in my mind:

....

....

....

....

....

....

....

This is the funniest dream I ever had:.................................

....

....

....

....

....

A TRIP BACK IN TIME

My favorite person in history is ....

If I could talk to this person, this is what I imagine

we would say: ....

....

....

....

....

....

....

....

....

....

....

....

....

....

....

....

SEPTEMBER: LOOKING BACK

This is what made me laugh the hardest this month:

This is what made me the angriest:

I felt foolish when

This was the most exciting event of September:

These are the books I read:

I enjoyed these movies:

Here's what happened at an after-school event:

This is something new that I learned this month:

On a scale of one to ten, I would rate this month a:

| 1 | 2 | 3 | 4 | 5 | 6 | 7 | 8 | 9 | 10 |

NEXT MONTH: LOOKING FORWARD

These are dates I want to remember next month:

Birthdays: ....

....

School events: ....

....

Holidays: ....

....

Other important dates: ....

....

This is something I'm looking forward to next month:

....

....

This is something coming up that I'm worried about:

....

....

This is something new I want to try next month: ....

....

....

OCTOBER

Finally Ramona could stand her fear and loneliness no longer. She slipped out of bed and tiptoed into her sister's room.

"Ramona?" Beezus, too, was awake.

"I can't go to sleep," whispered Ramona.

"Neither can I," said Beezus. "Come on, get in bed with me."

This invitation was what Ramona had been hoping for. Gratefully she slipped beneath the covers and snuggled against her sister.

Ramona and Her Mother

At the end of October comes the scariest night of the year!

When I was little, this is what I was afraid of:

Now that I'm older, this is what frightens me most:

The time I was most frightened was when

TELLING STORIES

Next to stories with lots of noise, Ramona liked stories about witches, goblins, or ogres.

Beezus and Ramona

The stories I like best are about:

- ☐ Witches or monsters
- ☐ Animals
- ☐ Someone like me
- ☐ Spaceships and planets
- ☐ Famous people
- ☐ Sports
- ☐ Foreign lands
- ☐ Historical events
- ☐ Romance
- ☐ Fairies and goblins
- ☐ Adventures
- ☐ Other

When I was little my favorite books were

The best book I read recently was

THE TOOTH FAIRY

Ramona had her suspicions about the tooth fairy.

Ramona the Pest

I have lost _____ baby teeth.
When I get a loose tooth, I:

- ☐ Leave it alone
- ☐ Jiggle it constantly
- ☐ Tie a string around it and yank
- ☐ Bleed a lot
- ☐ Put it under my pillow
- ☐ Receive _____ ¢ for it
- ☐ Keep it in a box
- ☐ Take it to school
- ☐ Other _____

SCHOOL'S IN

"I can't spell," said Ramona. "I'm terrible at spelling."

Ramona learned right there that Mrs. Rudge was a teacher who did not accept excuses. "There is no such word as *can't*," she said, and went on to inspect Becky's word sheet.

Ramona and Her Mother

I am a good/bad speller.
(circle one)

I am good/bad at remembering dates.

I am good/bad at math.

My best subject is

The subject I dislike most is

My teacher is very strict/easy. I think this is/isn't helpful because

SCHOOL'S OUT

Her afternoons after school seemed empty. Howie was home with tonsillitis, and she had no one to play with. She wished there were more children her age in her neighborhood. She was so lonely she picked up the telephone and dialed the Quimbys' telephone number to see if she could answer herself.

Ramona and Her Father

After school I usually do this:

I like most of all to

When I'm lonely, I do this:

These are the friends from my neighborhood I play with:

GOOD NEWS

Here's the best news I've heard recently: ....
....
....

This is good news I hope I'll hear soon: ....
....
....

She knew her father was singing about her, and in spite of her troubles Ramona found comfort in being her father's spunky gal.

Ramona the Brave

"A ghost could ooze in between the nails," whispered Beezus.

"A cold clammy ghost," agreed Ramona with a delicious shiver.

"A cold clammy ghost that sobbed in the night," elaborated Beezus, "and had icy fingers that—"

Ramona the Brave

Invent your own ghost story and write it down here:

She wrapped her arms around her knees to keep warm as she watched a dried leaf scratch along the driveway in the autumn wind.

Ramona and Her Father

Quiet moments are perfect for memories and serious thoughts.

This is my best memory:

This is something I've been thinking seriously about lately:

"Did I have tantrums, too?" Beezus asked.

"Once in a while," said Mother. "I always dreaded cutting your fingernails, because you kicked and screamed."

Beezus and Ramona

I want to kick and scream when

I had a tantrum once when

MY ROOM

Ramona stood inside her new closet, pretending she was in an elevator. She slid open the door and stepped out into her new room, which she pretended was on the tenth floor.

Ramona the Brave

This is the way my room looks:...

....

....

....

....

....

This is the way grown-ups think it should look:.........................

....

....

....

....

....

HALLOWEEN HAUNTING

"Make it a bad mask, Mama," she said. "I want to be the baddest witch in the whole world."

Ramona the Pest

This Halloween I: (Check the ones that are true for you.)

☐ Trick-or-treated
☐ Marched in a parade
☐ Went to a costume party
☐ Carved a jack-o'-lantern
☐ Told a scary story
☐ Drew a scary picture to hang in the window or on the door

These are some of the best costumes I saw this year:

....

....

....

....

Next year I want to dress up like:...................................

....

....

....

OCTOBER: LOOKING BACK

Here's something that I wish I'd done differently this month:

I'm proud of myself for doing this:

This is the song I liked best in October:

The best book I read this month was

The biggest news in school was

The person who pleased me most this month was

because

The best surprise of this month was

On a scale of one to ten, I would rate this month a:

| 1 | 2 | 3 | 4 | 5 | 6 | 7 | 8 | 9 | 10 |

NEXT MONTH: LOOKING FORWARD

These are dates I want to remember next month:

Birthdays:

School events:

Holidays:

Other important dates:

This is something I'm looking forward to next month:

This is something coming up that I'm worried about:

This is something new I want to try next month:

NOVEMBER

. . . before long dinner was on the table. Mother lit the candles and turned off the dining-room light. How pretty everything looks, thought Beezus. I wish we had candles on the table every night.

Beezus and Ramona

Thanksgiving comes in November. It's a time for dressing up like the Pilgrims and American Indians and for sharing a delicious meal with family and friends!

Here's what we ate for Thanksgiving dinner this year:

These are the people we celebrated Thanksgiving with this year:

This is a play or show my school put on to celebrate Thanksgiving:

WONDERFUL WORDS

Ramona was telling how her teacher had explained that the class should not be afraid of big words because big words were often made up of little words: *Dishcloth* meant a cloth for washing dishes and *pancake* meant a cake cooked in a pan.

"But I bake cakes in pans—or used to—and this does not make them pancakes," Mrs. Quimby pointed out. . . .

"I know," said Ramona. "I don't understand it because *carpet* does not mean a pet that rides in a car. Picky-picky is not a carpet when we take him to the vet."

Ramona and Her Mother

Here are some words I always used to misspell:

I think this would be a more sensible way to spell these words:

FUNNY TIME

Here's something I read in the newspaper that made me laugh:

WHAT'S COOKING?

The meal was a success. If the chicken did not taste as good as the girls had hoped and the corn bread did not rise like their mother's, both were edible. Beezus and Ramona were silently grateful to their parents for enjoying—or pretending to enjoy—their cooking. The whole family cheered up.

Ramona Quimby, Age 8

Cooking can be fun. Try making the Quimbys' Handy Dessert on page 192.

These are the foods I know how to prepare:......................

....

....

....

....

I do/don't like to cook. I also do/don't like to bake.
(circle one)
This is how I learned to cook:...................................

....

....

....

The biggest disaster that ever took place in our kitchen
was when

Ramona says, "Yummy!" and can make this delicious dessert herself. The rest of the family enjoys it, too.

The Quimbys' Handy Dessert

¾ cup graham cracker crumbs
1 14-ounce can of condensed milk, thoroughly chilled
¾ cup sugar
1 banana, mashed
   juice of two lemons

To make crumbs, put seven graham crackers in a plastic bag and crush with a rolling pin, or use a blender. Put the crumbs in a measuring cup to be sure they equal about ¾ cup. Spread half of the crumbs over the bottom of a 9-inch square pan.

Using an egg beater or an electric mixer, whip chilled condensed milk until stiff. Add the sugar, banana, and lemon juice. Mix well and spread over crumbs in pan. Sprinkle the rest of the crumbs over the mixture and freeze. Cut in squares to serve.

Bits of grated chocolate may be added to the condensed milk, banana, and lemon mixture. Crushed fruit that is not too juicy may be substituted for the banana.

PARENTS

The sisters scowled. They liked to cook; they did not like to be punished. They sat in silence, thinking cross thoughts about parents, especially their parents, their unfair, unkind parents who did not appreciate what nice daughters they had. Lots of parents would be happy to have nice daughters like Beezus and Ramona.

Ramona Quimby, Age 8

I think my parents should be happy to have a son/daughter like me because

HAPPY HOURS

This made me feel really happy:

Here's what I did to show how good I felt:

College, to Ramona, was a faraway school for young grown-ups. . . . Ramona was surprised to learn that she and her sister would be expected to go to such a school someday.

Ramona and Her Mother

Arguing with Ramona was a waste of time. So was appealing to her better nature. The best thing to do with Ramona, Beezus had learned, was to think up something to take the place of whatever her mind was fixed upon.

Beezus and Ramona

>>

She felt safe, knowing her mother was watching over her.

Ramona Quimby, Age 8

My mother or father makes me feel safe when

Miss Binney's face turned red and she looked so embarrassed that Ramona felt completely confused. Teachers were not supposed to look that way.

Ramona the Pest

My teacher once looked embarrassed when

I was once embarrassed when

IF I COULD . . .

If I could have one wish granted, this is what it would

be:

STUFFED WITH TURKEY

Leftovers—yuck!—thought Ramona. "Maybe Daddy will take us to Whopperburger for supper for payday," she said.

Ramona and Her Father

After Thanksgiving, we sometimes eat turkey leftovers all week long. There were/were not lots of leftovers this year.

If I could have Thanksgiving with a family from a book, this is what it would be like:..

....

....

....

....

....

....

....

NOVEMBER: LOOKING BACK

This is what made me laugh the hardest this month:

....

This is what made me the angriest:.......................................

....

I felt foolish when..

....

This was the most exciting event of November:...........................

....

These are the books I read:..

....

I enjoyed these movies:..

....

Here's what happened at an after-school event:..........................

....

This is something new that I learned this month:........................

....

....

On a scale of one to ten, I would rate this month a:

1   2   3   4   5   6   7   8   9   10

NEXT MONTH: LOOKING FORWARD

These are dates I want to remember next month:

Birthdays:..

....

School events:..

....

Holidays:...

....

Other important dates:...

....

This is something I'm looking forward to next month:

....

....

This is something coming up that I'm worried about:

....

....

This is something new I want to try next month:...........

....

DECEMBER

Ramona could not understand why grown-ups always talked about how quickly children grew up. Ramona thought growing up was the slowest thing there was, slower even than waiting for Christmas to come.

Ramona the Pest

December is filled with holiday happenings. It's the season of lights, love, and the spirit of giving.

This is how my family prepares for the Christmas or

Chanukah holidays:

For me, the really important thing about this holiday

is

FAMILY FLARE-UPS

Ramona heaved a sigh that seemed to come from the soles of her feet. In the bedroom, Beezus, who had run out of real sobs, was working hard to force out fake sobs to show her parents how mean they were to her.

Ramona Quimby, Age 8

The time I think my parents were meanest was when

....

....

....

....

When I want my parents to know I think they've been mean, this is what I do:....................................

....

....

....

....

"Please, Mother, I'll do anything you want if you'll let me go."

Ramona and Her Mother

My parents don't allow me to ....

because ....

....

....

....

....

....

....

....

....

....

....

....

....

SCHOOL'S IN

This was the silliest prank a classmate pulled in school
this month:

....

....

This was the most boring assignment we had to do:

....

....

Here's what my school did to celebrate the holiday
season:

....

....

Beezus felt a little better. She curled up on the davenport again with *202 Things to Do on a Rainy Afternoon* and read about making Christmas-tree ornaments out of cellophane straws, until she heard her aunt's car turn into the driveway. Then she flung her book aside and ran out to greet her.

Beezus and Ramona

"I won't get over it!" Nobody had to tell Ramona that life was full of disappointments. She already knew.

Ramona and Her Mother

Ramona was surprised. She had never been called adorable before. Bright, lively, yes; adorable, no. She smiled and felt more lovable.

Ramona and Her Father

ME ON THE INSIDE

If only she had some imagination, like Ramona—but no, Miss Robbins said everybody had imagination. Well, if she had imagination, where was it?

Beezus and Ramona

One time when I thought, like Beezus, that I had no imagination was

But a time I showed real imagination was when

IF I COULD . . .

If I worked hard, maybe someday I could become

....

....

I would like to do this because ....

....

....

....

....

....

....

....

....

....

....

HAPPY HOURS

This made me feel really happy: ....

....

....

....

....

....

Here's what I did to show how good I felt: ....

....

....

....

....

....

HOLIDAY MEMORIES

They would look at Ramona in her new red-and-green-plaid slacks and red turtleneck sweater and say, Ramona is one of Santa's helpers, a regular little Christmas elf.

Ramona and Her Mother

These are the gifts I received for Christmas or Chanukah: ....

....

....

....

I wrote thank-you letters to ....

....

....

I was happy because ....

....

....

This is what was nicest about the holiday:

....

DECEMBER: LOOKING BACK

Here's something that I wish I'd done differently this

month: ....

....

I'm proud of myself for doing this: ....

....

This is the song I liked best in December: ....

....

The best book I read this month was ....

....

The biggest news in school was ....

....

The person who pleased me the most this month was

....

because ....

....

The best surprise of this month was ....

....

On a scale of one to ten, I would rate this month a:

1   2   3   4   5   6   7   8   9   10

NEXT MONTH: LOOKING FORWARD

These are dates I want to remember next month:

Birthdays:

School events:

Holidays:

Other important dates:

This is something I'm looking forward to next month:

This is something coming up that I'm worried about:

This is something new I want to try next month:

MY YEAR: LOOKING BACK

"Isn't it funny?" she remarked as her father steered the car into their driveway.

"Isn't what funny?" asked her mother.

"That I used to be little and funny-looking and cross-eyed like Roberta," said Ramona. "And now look at me. I'm wonderful me!"

"Except when you're blunderful you," said Beezus.

Ramona did not mind when her family, except Roberta, who was too little, laughed. "Yup, wonderful, blunderful me," she said and was happy. She was winning at growing up.

Ramona Forever

Well, you've done it. You've made it through another whole year full of ups and downs. You probably don't even realize all the wonderful ways in which you've changed and grown, but if you look back at the beginning pages of your diary, you're sure to find at least a few. These next pages are a good place to take stock of all the different ways in which you, like Ramona, are "winning at growing up."

Since I began this diary, I have grown .... inches

and gained/lost .... pounds.
(circle one)

I am now .... feet .... inches tall and weigh .... pounds.

I look different in these other ways:...............

....

....

The books I read now are different in this way:...............

....

....

The music I enjoy is different in this way:...............

....

....

My personality is a little different because I am less

....

and more ....

....

I no longer worry about...............

....

The area in which I have grown up the most is...............

....

NEXT YEAR:
LOOKING FORWARD

Next year I want to change this about myself:

I want to break this habit:

I'd like to be nicer to this person:

And I'm going to tell
to be nicer to me.

I want to learn to do this:

But I don't want to ever change this about myself:

I will keep this diary to read when I grow up.
Signed *Elizabeth Rangel Konir*